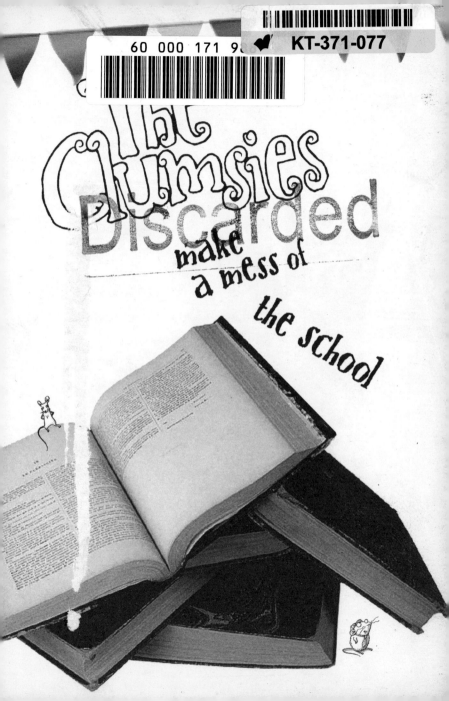

The Clumsies

Discarded

make
a mess of

the school

First published in paperback in Great Britain
by HarperCollins Children's Books in 2011
HarperCollins Children's Books is a division
of HarperCollinsPublishers Ltd
77-85 Fulham Palace Road,
Hammersmith, London W6 8JB

Visit us on the web at
www.harpercollins.co.uk

1

Text copyright © Sorrel Anderson 2011
Illustrations copyright © Nicola Slater 2011

ISBN: 978-0-00-743867-9

Printed and bound in England
by Clays Ltd, St Ives plc

MIX
Paper from
responsible sources
FSC® C007454
www.fsc.org

FSC is a non-profit international organisation established to promote the
responsible management of the world's forests. Products carrying the FSC
label are independently certified to assure consumers that they come
from forests that are managed to meet the social, economic and
ecological needs of present and future generations.

Find out more about HarperCollins and the environment at
www.harpercollins.co.uk/green

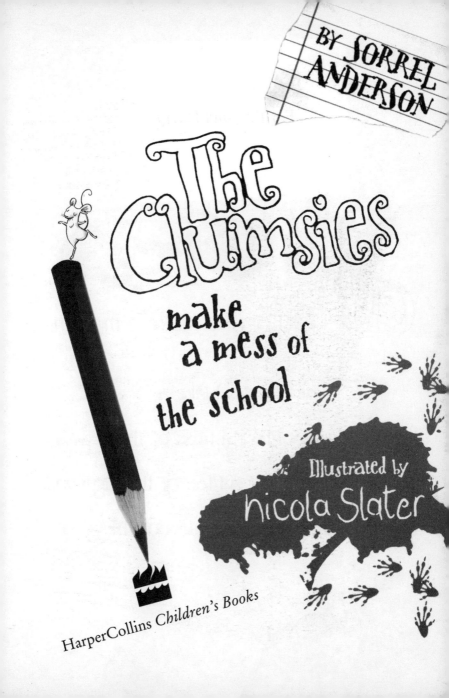

BY SORREL ANDERSON

The Clumsies

make a mess of the school

Illustrated by
nicola Slater

HarperCollins Children's Books

The Clumsies also make a mess in:

The Clumsies Make a Mess

The Clumsies Make a Mess of the Seaside

The Clumsies Make a Mess of the Big Show

The Clumsies Make a Mess of the Zoo

Contents

ST.
APRICOTS

It was a Tuesday morning and the Clumsies were hiding under the desk while Mr Bullerton - Howard's boss - was *looming* over it, **shouting** at Howard.

'I wonder what Howard's done now?' whispered Purvis, to Mickey Thompson.

'I don't know,' whispered Mickey Thompson, back, 'but whatever it is I wish they'd hurry up.

I want my breakfast.'

'**TOOT**,' agreed Ortrud, **loudly**.

'*Shhh,*' whispered Purvis.

'Listen: he's saying something about a…'

'School?' said Howard.

'School' confirmed Mr Bullerton.

'But I don't want to go to

School ,' said Howard. 'I've already done all that; I'm an adult now.'

Mr Bullerton snorted

'You will go to that School up the road,' he said, gesturing, 'and you'll give them a message from me.'

'You don't mean St Apricot's?' asked Howard.

'I do mean St Apricot's,' said Mr Bullerton. 'They're having a GRAND SPORTS DAY this afternoon, so I've decided to attend as Guest of Honour. The people there will notice me and be impressed. That's the first part of the message.'

'But…' began Howard.

'And you may tell them,' continued Mr Bullerton, **puffing** out his chest, 'that even though I am a busy and important person with a busy and important schedule, I shall kindly make time to give them a speech and hand out

the prizes. My name will be
famous! That's the second part
of the message.'

'But have they invited you?'
asked Howard. 'Surely you'd
need to be invited?'

'Nonsense,' said Mr
Bullerton. 'They're lucky to
have me, and you can tell them
that too, as part three.'

'I see,' said Howard.

'And *then*,' continued Mr
Bullerton, again, 'you must
put in place the appropriate

arrangements.'

'How do you mean?' said Howard.

Mr Bullerton **_tutted_**. 'The usual things for a Guest of Honour, of course,' he said. 'Plinths, cordials, etc.'

'Eh?' said Howard.

'I SAID PLINTHS, CORDIALS, ETC,'

shouted Mr Bullerton.

'Make sure they're

ready. Go on, then; off you go.'

'Can't it wait a little while?' asked Howard. 'Only there are one or two things I need to…'

'GO!'

shouted Mr Bullerton, and Howard leapt up and dived under the desk.

'Howard!' *gasped* the mice.

'HOWARD ARMITAGE!!!'

roared Mr Bullerton.

'Help,' gulped Howard.

'Of course,' said the mice.
'We'll come with you.'

'No you won't,' said
Howard. 'Not this time.'

'WHAT?'

shouted Mr Bullerton.

'WHAT ARE YOU
DOING UNDER

THERE?'

'I'm err… err…'

'Finding your bag,' whispered Purvis,

handing Howard an

enormous

bag, and climbing into it.

Mickey Thompson and Ortrud

climbed in too.

'I SAID NO,' **shouted** Howard.

'DON'T YOU "NO" ME!' **shouted** Mr Bullerton. 'COME OUT AT ONCE!'

Howard sighed, defeatedly, grasped the bag tightly, and stood up.

'Sorry about that,' he said, sidling towards the door. 'I was just finding my bag.'

Mr Bullerton stared at it.

'It's **enormous**,' he said.

'Is it?' said Howard, sidling faster. 'I hadn't noticed.'

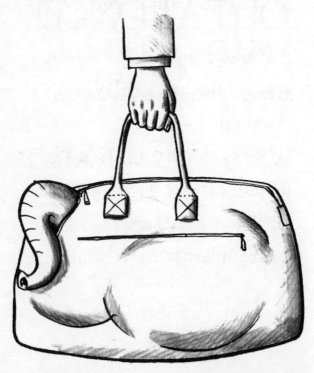

'What's in it?' said Mr Bullerton.

'*Err*, nothing,' said Howard, whisking out of the room and racing down the corridor towards the lift.

'WHAT?' **shouted** Mr Bullerton. 'WAIT! I DON'T WANT YOU MUCKING ANYTHING UP THIS TIME, HOWARD ARMITAGE!'

'No, bye,' waved Howard, as the lift arrived with a 'PING!' and he hurried inside. '**DID YOU HEAR WHAT I SAID?**' *yelled* Mr Bullerton, as the doors clunked shut. '*Where to?*' said the lift.

'Come along, come along,' said Howard, jabbing the buttons.

'*Ask nicely, now,*' giggled the lift, not budging. 'Say the magic word.'

'What's the matter with it?' said Howard, jabbing harder.

'*La, la, la,*' went the lift, humming to itself.

There was a scrabbling noise from inside the bag and Purvis peeped out.

'It's us,' he said to the lift. 'Ground

floor, please.'

'Delighted to oblige,' said the lift, setting off.

'At last,' muttered Howard.

'He's agitated,' observed the lift, as they trundled down. 'What's afoot?'

'We're taking a complicated message to the

 message to the

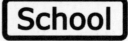

up the road,' said Purvis.

'They're having a

GRAND
SPORTS DAY.'

'Ooh!' said the lift. 'I've
heard about those: there'll be
people running and leaping
about and all sorts. Some of
them get into sacks and bounce
around.'

There was another scrabbling
noise from inside the bag and
Mickey Thompson peeped out,

looking surprised.

'It's true!' said the lift, warming to its theme. 'There's even a race where one person gets tied onto another person and they c h a r g e

up
and
down, or fall over,

more like. It wouldn't be my cup of tea but they enjoy it.'

'Mr Bullerton's decided to be the Guest of Honour,' said Purvis.

'Has he, now?' said the lift. 'Got him in that great  **big** bag, have you?'

'No,' said Purvis. 'He's following on later once we've put in place the appropriate arrangements.'

'Those being?'
said the lift.

'The usual things
for a Guest of
Honour,' explained
Mickey Thompson.

'That's a big
responsibility,' the
lift told them, as
they landed with a
b^{um}p and the doors
pinged open.
'Let's hope nothing
goes wrong.'

'At last,' said Howard, hurrying out. 'It gives me the *heebie-jeebies* when you talk to that thing. Lifts aren't supposed to talk.'

'Neither are mice,' pointed out Mickey Thompson, **cheerfully**, 'but that doesn't stop you talking to us.'

'That's different,' said Howard.

'Why?' said Mickey Thompson.

'It just is,' said Howard.

'But…' began Mickey Thompson.

'There isn't time to discuss it now,' said Howard, quickly. 'We need to get going.'

'But…' began Mickey Thompson, again.

'We can collect my dog on the way,' said Howard. 'The road to the School passes right by my house.'

'Allen!' **cheered** the mice.

'Allen,' agreed Howard.

'He'll enjoy the walk, and Mr Bullerton need never know.'

So the Clumsies nestled back down in the bag, Howard hoisted it over his shoulder  and, collecting Allen on the way, they set off up the road past offices and shops and a fence and a park and a wall and some houses and trees, and eventually they arrived at the **School** .

Howard stopped.

'Now listen,' he said. 'Best behaviour, understand?'

There was no reply.

'Do you understand me?' he said.

There was still no reply so Howard put the bag down and **peered inside**.

Mickey Thompson and Purvis

**peered
back up
at him.**

'Well?' said Howard.

'What?' they said.

'Did you hear what I said?' said Howard.

'No,' they said.

'There's a lot of traffic and birds and things,' said Purvis.

'I was saying,' said Howard, 'you're to be on your best behaviour.'

'PARDON?'

shouted Mickey Thompson.

Howard ignored him. 'I
don't want any... you know...
incidents.'

'Of course not, Howard,'
said the mice.

'And no mess,' said Howard.
'Absolutely none.'

'No, Howard,' said the mice.

'And I'm including Ortrud
in this,' said Howard, firmly.
'Does she understand?' There
was a loud snore from inside
the bag.

'She's sleeping, Howard,'

said Purvis. 'We'll explain it to her later.'

'Make sure you do,' said Howard. 'Now, Allen had better wait out here,' he said, settling Allen in a comfortable spot. 'We won't be long.'

He hoisted the bag up again, trudged into the School and staggered backwards as a woman whizzed past on a small silver scooter, narrowly missing him.

'Oof,' he said.

'WHEE!' **shouted**
the woman. 'WATCH
YOURSELF, LADDIE!'
She skidded to a halt and
dismounted. 'They're not

allowed to ride them in the corridors so I've confiscated it, temporarily,' she said, tapping the scooter. 'But I couldn't resist a little go; they are my corridors, after all.'

'Are they?' said Howard, sounding surprised.

'In a manner of speaking,' said the woman. 'I am the Headmistress of this establishment: JB Undercracker, at your service.' She clicked her heels and thrust out a hand, so

Howard shook it.

'Right,' said **JB Undercracker**, briskly. 'Who are you and what do you want?'

'I've come with a message,' said Howard.

'Oh yes?' said **JB Undercracker**.

'Actually, several,' said Howard.

'Oh yes?' said **JB Undercracker**.

'Actually one, but it's got several parts,' said Howard.

JB Undercracker **narrowed** her eyes.

'Spill,' she said.

'Sorry?' said Howard.

'The beans, sonny,' said **JB Undercracker**. 'Spill 'em.'

'Right,' said Howard. 'Well, it's Mr Bullerton...'

'Delighted to meet you, Mr Bullerton,' said **JB Undercracker**.

'No, no,' said Howard. 'I...'

'We are making good progress, aren't we?' she said. 'And now we've established the *who you are* part of the equation, let's tackle the *what do you want*. To what do we owe the pleasure?'

Howard mopped his brow. 'It's about your

GRAND SPORTS DAY,'

he said.

'*AAGGH!*' she *shrieked*, and Howard jumped. 'We're so excited.

The children have been preparing for WEEKS.'

'That's good,' said Howard, 'because he, Mr Bullerton I mean, the real one, not me, is going to be St Apricot's Guest of Honour.'

'Super. Now look at this,' said **JB Undercracker**, fiddling with the scooter. 'It's got a very interesting mechanism.'

'*Err*, yes,' said Howard. 'So as I was saying, he's

importantly making some time for a speech and, and prizes and… busy schedule…'

'I've always wondered how these things worked,' said **JB Undercracker**, spinning the wheel.

'That was parts one and two of the message,' said Howard, pressing on, 'and part three was to tell you you're lucky.'

'Aren't we just,' said **JB Undercracker**, beaming. 'Is that everything?'

'I think so,' said Howard.

'No, it isn't,' hissed Purvis, from inside the bag. 'You've forgotten the plinths, cordials etc.'

'OH, YES!'

shouted Howard, 'I nearly forgot. We'll be needing some plinths and cordials.'

'*Plinths?*' said JB Undercracker.

'And cordials,' nodded Howard.

'Etc,' hissed Purvis.

'Shhh,' hissed Howard, hurriedly stuffing the bag behind his back. JB Undercracker gave him a funny look.

'There might be a bottle of orange squash in the kitchen,' she said. 'Would that be of any use?'

'It's a start,' said Howard.

'Or I'll tell you what, how about a nice cup of tea instead? You look as though you could do with one.'

'Yes please,' croaked
Howard.

'Good man,' said **JB
Undercracker**, slapping him
on the back. 'Leave the bag in
my office and come with me.'

'I'd prefer to keep hold of it,

thank you,' said Howard.

'Nonsense,' said **JB**
Undercracker. 'It's far too
big. What's in it?'

'NOTHING,'
shouted Howard.
'Nothing at all.'

'Well in that case you won't
be needing it, will you?' she
said, wrestling it from him, and
flinging it into a nearby room.
'Come along, Mr Bullerton.'
She climbed onto the scooter
and shot off up the corridor,

with Howard trotting worriedly behind.

'**OUch,**' said the mice, and '**TOOT,**' went Ortrud, as the big bag landed with a bump on the floor of **JB Undercracker**'s office.

Mickey Thompson heaved a

disappointed-sounding sigh.

'What's the matter?' asked
Purvis.

'Well, if they've gone for a
cup of tea they'll probably be
having a biscuit or something,
won't they?' he said.

'Possibly,' said Purvis.

'Or a slice of cake.'

'You never know,' said Purvis.

'Or a little sandwich, even.'

'Your point being?' said Purvis.

'We won't get any,' said Mickey Thompson. 'And we didn't have any breakfast. And I'm hungry.'

'**TOOT**,' went Ortrud.

'Me too, now you mention it,' said Purvis. 'Let's have a look around: maybe **JB Undercracker**'s got a biscuit tin.'

So they all climbed out of
the bag and had a look around.
They searched through the
cupboards, rummaged amongst
the bookshelves, explored

under the desk and checked
behind each and every one

of **JB Undercracker**'s nick-knacks, photographs and certificates, but there was no biscuit tin.

'Bother,' said Mickey Thompson.

'Oh well, I don't suppose Howard will be much longer,' said Purvis. 'We can ask him to take us all for a café lunch before we go back to the office.'

'But I need something now,' groaned Mickey Thompson, clutching his tummy. 'I'm

feeling dreadfully faint.' He
staggered dramatically
and collapsed
against a
nearby vase.

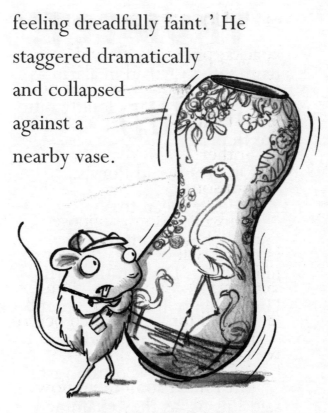

'CAREFUL!' **shouted**

Purvis, as it toppled.

'TRUMPET!'

trumpeted Ortrud in alarm as
it CRASHED loudly onto
the floor.

'Oh dear,' said Purvis.

'I didn't mean to,'
said Mickey Thompson,
unhappily. 'Do you think JB
Underthingy'll be very upset?'

'I expect that depends on
how fond she was of the vase,'
said Purvis, as they examined
the broken pieces.

'The pattern was pretty,' said

Mickey Thompson, even more
unhappily. 'I'd have been fond
of it, if it had been mine.'

'Don't worry,' said Purvis.
'The bits are quite big. We
could probably glue them
together…'

'Ooh!' said Mickey
Thompson, brightening.

'If we had some glue.'

'Ah,' said Mickey Thompson,
deflating. 'I don't remember
seeing any when we were going
through everything just now.'

'It's easy to miss glue if you're looking for biscuits,' said Purvis. 'Let's double check, quick.' So they frantically scrabbled back through the photos and nick-knacks and cupboards and books and everything under the desk, but there was no glue.

'Oh, oh,' said Mickey Thompson. 'Oh.'

'Don't panic,' said Purvis. 'Help! Help!' said Mickey Thompson, starting to.

'Come on,' said Purvis. 'This is a great big building; there's bound to be some glue in it somewhere. Let's hurry and find it before they get back.' He climbed onto Ortrud, *yanked* Mickey Thompson up after him, and they galloped off.

'TRUMPET!'

went Ortrud, excitedly, as they careered down the corridors.

'Faster!' puffed Purvis.

'STOP!' *yelled* Mickey Thompson.

Ortrud skidded to a halt and the mice fell off.

'OUCH,' said Purvis. 'What did you do that for?'

'DINOSAURS!'

said Mickey Thompson, pointing into the distance. 'I can hear them!'

'It can't be,' said Purvis.

'Well there's definitely something there,' said Mickey Thompson, 'and it's coming this way. LISTEN.'

Glue
and
the
wall of
lunch

Mickey Thompson was right:
there was a rumbling in
the distance
like drums or thunder,
and it was… getting…
LOUDER.

'EEK!' squeaked the mice and '**TOOT**,' went Ortrud. They all bundled into a nearby room and flattened themselves against the floor just in time as what seemed like *hundreds* and

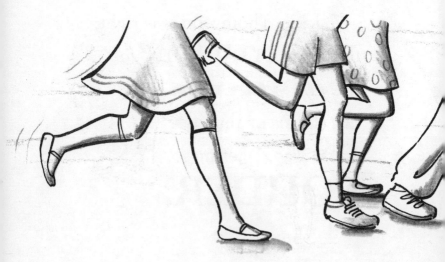

hundreds of shoes **stamped** past. Attached to the shoes were **hundreds** and **hundreds** of socks and attached to the socks were **hundreds** and **hundreds** of children.

'Wow,' said Mickey
Thompson, once they'd
disappeared
into the distance. 'Those
must have been the School
children.'

'I wasn't expecting so many,'
said Purvis.

'Nor that they'd go so
fast,' said Mickey Thompson.
'I wonder what made them
stampede like that.'

'I suppose something startled
them,' said Purvis, and Mickey

Thompson made a *groaning* noise.

'You're right,' he said. 'It was the crashing vase. Oh, what have I done? What have I done?'

'Eh?' said Purvis.

'It's all my fault,' said Mickey Thompson. 'I broke the vase that caused the crash that started the st**a**mp**e**d**e**.'

'Well, I don't think…' began
Purvis.

'And what if they can't
stop running and running and
eventually someone trips up
and falls down and gets hurt?
It'll all be because of me.'

'No, no,' said Purvis. 'I
really don't…'

'No, I really don't either,'
said a voice from somewhere
above. The mice ju^mped and
gazed around but there was no
one to be seen.

'Did you hear it?' mouthed
Mickey Thompson, at Purvis.

'Yes,' mouthed Purvis, back.

'Who said it?' mouthed
Mickey Thompson, at Purvis.

'I don't know,' mouthed
Purvis, back.

'Greetings, mice, and
elephant,' said the voice. 'I can
see you.'

'A ghost, an invisible ghost!'
shrieked Mickey Thompson,
grabbing onto Purvis.

'I am neither a ghost nor

invisible,' said the voice, calmly. 'I am Russell.'

They peered upwards again but there was still no one to be seen.

'On the table,' said Russell, helpfully.

'I'm going up,' said Purvis, starting to climb the table that was in the middle of the room.

'Wait!' said Mickey Thompson. 'We don't know what's up there.'

'It's Russell,' said Purvis. 'He

said so. Come on.'

So Purvis started climbing again, followed by Mickey Thompson and Ortrud.

'May I make a suggestion?' called Russell, as the table started to *creak* and **judder**.

'Please do,' called Purvis.

'It might be better if your small elephant waited on the floor.'

'Oh, OK,' said Purvis. 'Go on, then, Ortrud. We'll see you later.'

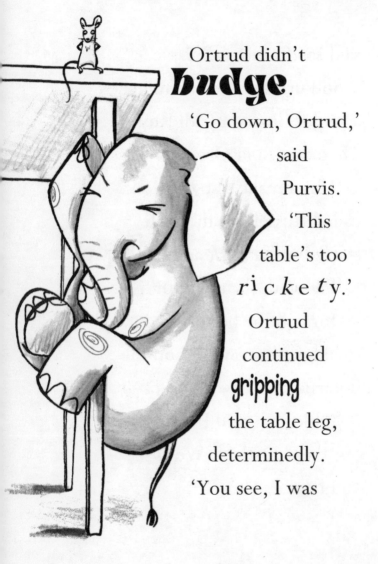

Ortrud didn't **budge**.

'Go down, Ortrud,' said Purvis. 'This table's too *rⁱckety*.' Ortrud continued **gripping** the table leg, determinedly. 'You see, I was

thinking we should have
someone trustworthy to guard
the door for us,' said Russell.
'We don't want anyone barging
in, do we?'

'He's got a point,' said
Mickey Thompson.

'How about it, Ortrud?' said
Purvis.

'TOOT,' went
Ortrud, and she let go of the
table leg, plunked to the floor

and ambled off to keep watch
while the others continued
upwards.

But when they reached the top
they found nothing but a glass
container and a scattering of
leaves and twigs.

'Is it some kind of nature-
study project, do you think?'
asked Purvis, nudging a piece of
greenery with his foot.

'It looks more like someone's
forgotten to sweep up,' said

Mickey Thompson. 'But where's Russell?'

'Here,' said one of the twigs, and Mickey Thompson's mouth fell open in surprise. 'Did you see that?' he said. 'That twig just talked. It's a talking twig.'

'Stick, actually,' said Russell, giving a little bow. 'Stick *insect*, that is. At your service.'

'Have you got any glue?' asked Mickey Thompson, and Purvis shushed him.

'What?' said Mickey Thompson.

'Sorry, Russell,' said Purvis.

'Why?' said Mickey Thompson.

'We've only just met him,'

hissed Purvis. 'You can't just go asking for stuff straight off like that, it isn't polite. We should have a little chit-chat first.'

'Oh,' said Mickey Thompson. 'Go on, then.'

Purvis cleared his throat. 'Hello, Russell,' he said. 'It's lovely to meet you.'

'You too,' said Russell.

'Me three,' said Mickey Thompson, quickly. 'Have you got any glue?'

Purvis sighed.

'We've broken JB
Undersomething's vase,'
announced Mickey Thompson.

'You mean you did,' muttered
Purvis,
and there was a
small scuffle.
'OK, OK,'
said Mickey
Thompson,
giving in. 'I mean *I* broke it.'

'Which one?' asked Russell.

'The big one with birds on,'

said Mickey Thompson.

'Ah, the flamingos,' said
Russell, nodding. 'Yes. She was
fond of that vase.'

Mickey Thompson started
to look worried again.

'We had a
feeling she
might
be,' said
Purvis.
'That's why
we need the
glue: we want

to fix it.'

'Was that the **big** crash I heard, earlier?' asked Russell.

'Probably,' said Purvis. 'And now Mickey Thompson's worried it set off the **stampede** and that he's to blame.'

Mickey Thompson nodded.

'Nonsense,' said Russell. 'Those children are always charging about like that. It's simply youthful exuberance.'

'Really?' said the mice.

'Really,' said Russell. 'So no more fretting: it wasn't your fault.'

'Phew,' said Mickey Thompson, *cheering up*.

'Unlike the vase,' said Russell, 'which, from the sound of it, was.'

'Hmm,' said Mickey Thompson,

clouding over.

'But never mind,' said
Russell, kindly. 'I know where
you can get some glue. Listen
carefully. Go out of this room,
turn left, turn right, turn left
again, keep going for quite a
long time, take another left,
and another right, keep going
some more and you'll come
to a door. That isn't the door
you want. Carry on past it and
you'll come to a different door
marked **ART ROOM**. That's
the place for glue; it's bursting

with the stuff.'

Mickey Thompson exhaled
sharply.

'Actually,' said Russell,
'while you're at it, could
you pick me up a tube of red
paint? I want to paint my egg
with it.' He pointed across
the table towards a large egg
that was tottering on top of a
complicated contraption made
from wire and rubber bands.

The mice stared at it.

'*Err*,' said Purvis.

'Cor,' said Mickey
Thompson.

'Do you like it?' said Russell.
'It's for one of the races this
afternoon.'

'Eh?' said Purvis.

'Oh,' said Mickey Thompson, 'I get it – you chuck them.'

'We do not "chuck them",' said Russell. 'We *race* them. Each contestant has to build a device that will carry their egg from point A to point B. The egg that gets the furthest is the winner.'

'Ah!' said Purvis. 'OK: one tube of red paint coming right up.'

'Thanks,' said Russell. 'Well, cheerio then. And good luck.'

'Um, just remind me,' said Purvis, 'was it left and then left or… err…'

'Shall I come with you and show you the way?' asked Russell.

'Yes, please,' said Purvis, sounding relieved, so they all set off down the table leg and climbed on to Ortrud, who was vigilantly guarding the door.

'Well, this is a new

experience,' commented Russell. 'I've never had a ride on an elephant before.'

'Oh, we do it all the time,' said Mickey Thompson, loftily, as they **trotted** along with Purvis sitting up front to help with the steering, and Russell calling out directions.

'I'll point out the places of interest,' said Russell.

'LIBRARY.'

'**Ooh,**' said Purvis, peering in through a window.

'GYMNASIUM,'

called Russell. 'And here are some CLASSROOMS: look at the drawings they've put up outside.'

'Lovely!' said Purvis.

'Staff room approaching,' said Russell, dropping his voice. 'It might be an idea to *speed* up here, in case someone springs out and tells us off. I'm not sure elephants are allowed in the corridors.'

Ortrud *sped* up.

'Nicely done,' said Russell, as they rounded the corner safely. 'Ah yes, and now we're entering the **PACKED LUNCH STORAGE AREA.**'

89

'What?' said Mickey Thompson. 'Where?'

'See all those shelves and compartments and boxes?' said Russell, pointing. 'That's where the children put their packed lunches for safekeeping.'

Mickey Thompson made a **gurgling** noise.

'What's in them?' he asked.

'Oh, the usual kind of thing,' said Russell. 'Sandwiches, wraps, dips, salady bits…'

Mickey Thompson made
another **gurgling** noise.

'…flasks of soup, leftovers from dinner the day before…'

'Can we stop a minute, please?' said Mickey Thompson.

'There isn't time,' said Purvis.

'Noodles,' said Russell, 'Fruit. Cold roast potatoes.'

'S T O P ! '

shouted Mickey Thompson.

'I NEED TO LOOK

AT THE WALL OF LUNCH!'

'No!' said Purvis. 'We must get the glue first. You can look later.'

'But, but…' splattered Mickey Thompson.

'And we're almost at our destination,' said Russell, as they passed the door they didn't want and arrived in front of the one marked

'ART ROOM'.

'Come,' he said,
and led the way
through a big white
studio cluttered with
easels and spattered
with paint and clay,
and over to a cupboard
marked, '*Adhesives, etc.*'
'Glue, etc.' said
Russell, opening
the cupboard
door to

reveal tubes and tubs and
bottles and jars of more kinds
of glue than Purvis had ever
imagined existed.

'Gosh,' he said.

'I know,' said Russell,
opening a drawer and finding
the red paint he wanted.

'Make sure you choose the
right one.'

'But how?' said Purvis.

'Well, for a start it'll need to
say "suitable for ceramics",' said
Russell. 'Otherwise the vase

won't stick.'

'Good point,' said Purvis.

'And do you prefer a thick glue or a thin one?'

'I'm not sure,' said Purvis. 'Is there anything mediumish?'

'I'd go for the thick if I were you,' said Russell. 'Clear or white?'

'*Err*, clear,' said Purvis.

'Smelly or not?'

'Not,' said Purvis.

'Fast or slow?'

'In what sense?' said Purvis.

'Drying time,' said Russell.
'Speed of adhesion, as it were.'

'Fast, definitely,' said Purvis,
glancing anxiously at the clock
on the studio wall.

'Squirter or brush?'

'Sorry?' said Purvis.

'Do you want to squirt it
on with a squirter or dab it
on with a brush?' said Russell.

'Oh, squirter I should think.'
said Purvis.

'I'd advise a brush,' said
Russell.

'OK,' said Purvis. 'Brush it is.'

'Right,' said Russell,
rummaging in the cupboard
and emerging with a huge and
rather sticky-looking pot of
glue. 'This is the one.'

'Thank you,' said Purvis,

taking it. '*Err*… eugh… we'd better get going. ORTRUD! WE'RE READY.'

So Ortrud, who had wandered away to look at some paintings, trotted over and Purvis and Russell climbed on.

'We appear to be missing someone,' said Russell.

'*Tut,*' said Purvis. 'Where's he gone now?'

'Hmm,' said Russell.

'Oh no,' said Purvis. 'You don't think…'

'It's a distinct possibility,'
said Russell.

'QUICK!'

shouted Purvis. 'WE
MUST FIND HIM
BEFORE HE GETS
INTO ANY MORE
TROUBLE!'

Trumpeting urgently,
Ortrud galloped through the
studio, crashing into easels and
knocking over pots of paint.

'AAGH!'
shouted Purvis as
they slipped and *skidded*

through puddles of red and
yellow and orange and blue
and, eventually, muddy brown.
'WE'RE LEAVING
FOOTPRINTS
EVERYWHERE!'
'We can come back and wipe
them up later,' said Russell,
as they passed the door they
didn't want and cantered down
the corridor towards the wall of
lunch.

'Yikes!' squeaked Purvis,
when they reached it. 'Look.'

There were open lunchboxes
scattered everywhere and
the shelves and the floor
were covered in half-eaten
sandwiches and blobs of soup
and strands of noodle and slices
of fruit, and in the middle
of the mayhem sat Mickey
Thompson, with a look of
strong concentration, eating a
cold roast potato.

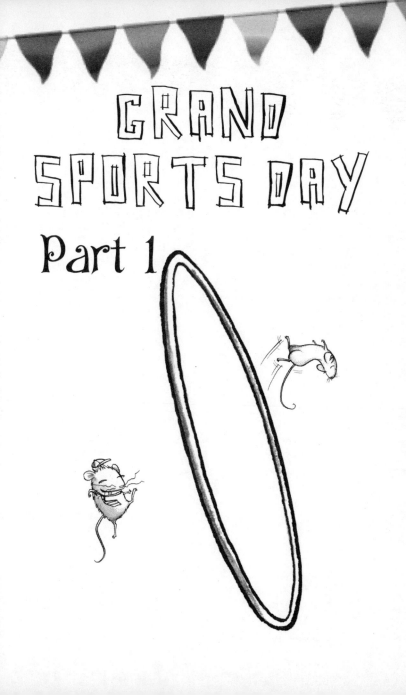

GRAND SPORTS DAY

Part 1

shouted Purvis, as
they approached.

'MICKEY
THOMPSON!'
shouted Howard,
as he approached from the
opposite direction.

'Oh, hello there,' said
Mickey Thompson, trying to
appear casual.

'What have you done?'
whimpered Howard, arriving,
and gazing around at the mess.

'Err, ooooh,' said
Mickey Thompson, noticing it
for the first time. 'I was just
having a look.'

'In every box!' said Howard.

Mickey Thompson nodded,
guiltily.

'And eating the food,' said

Howard. 'Which you shouldn't have been: it isn't yours.'

'I only took a tiny taste from each one,' said Mickey Thompson. 'I thought it would be fairer that way, and less noticeable.'

'Less noticeable, he says,' said Howard. 'I'm yet to see something resembling anything less unnoticeable than this!!!' said Howard, gesticulating wildly.

'Sorry, Howard,' said Mickey
Thompson. 'Here: try one of
these.' He offered Howard a
cold roast potato and Howard
took it, and ate it.

'*Err,* Howard,' said Purvis.

'What?' said Howard.

'Mmm. These are lovely. Are
there any more?'

'Lots,' said Mickey
Thompson, handing

another one over, and taking
one for himself.

'*Err*, Howard,' said Purvis,
again. 'Don't you think we
ought to try and do something
about the mess?'

'Mmm?' said Howard. 'Oh
yes, and that's another thing.
What on earth happened in **JB
Undercracker**'s office?'

'Cracker!' said Mickey
Thompson. 'That was it!'

'No thanks,' said Howard,
'but I'll have another potato
if there's one going spare.'
Mickey Thompson handed him
another one.

'Do you mean the vase,
Howard?' asked Purvis.

'I mean the everything,' said
Howard. 'The whole room's

been turned upside down. She
thinks she's been burgled.'

'*Oh-err*,' said Purvis.

'Quite,' said Howard. 'Care
to offer an explanation?'

'We were looking for glue
to mend the vase that broke
because we couldn't find the
biscuit tin,' explained Purvis.

Howard frowned at him,
confusedly.

'It was all because we didn't
have any breakfast,' added
Purvis, with a small *sigh*.

Howard continued frowning.

'What's up?' asked Purvis.

'I think I need another
potato,' said Howard, and
Mickey Thompson passed him
one.

'Thanks,' said Howard,
clearing himself a space
amongst the debris and settling
down on the floor to eat it.

'Budge over a bit,' he said,

to Mickey Thompson. 'Is there anything to drink?'

'Would you prefer blackcurrant, or mountain water with a hint of lime?' asked Mickey Thompson, waving a couple of cartons.

'Lime, please,' said Howard, and Mickey Thompson handed it over, with another potato.

'Excuse me,' whispered Russell. 'I don't like to interrupt but I think I hear the sound of an oncoming scooter.'

Russell was right. It was **JB Undercracker**, whizzing up the corridor towards them.

The mice dived into the
nearest lunchbox, pulling
Russell after them, and Ortrud
hid in a doorway.

'What are you doing?' said
Howard, to the mice.

'What are *you* doing,
Mr Bullerton?' said JB
Undercracker, arriving, and
skidding to a halt.

'EEK,' said Howard,
jumping. 'Hello JB… I mean
Miss… I mean Mrs… I
mean…'

'JB will do nicely,' said **JB Undercracker**. 'Now listen, laddie. I don't mean to be inhospitable. I hope that's understood.'

'Absolutely,' said Howard.

'St Apricot's is renowned for its hospitableness,' said **JB Undercracker**.

'Far and wide,' said Howard. 'I've heard it mentioned often.'

'Then the situation is even better than I thought,' she said. 'But the thing is, these are the children's lunches.'

'Yes,' said Howard, nodding his head in agreement.

'Which means they belong to the *children*,' emphasised **JB Undercracker**. 'They're not intended for consumption by Mr Bullertons and other members of the general public.'

'No,' said Howard, shaking his head in agreement.

'Then why are you?' said **JB Undercracker**.

'I'm not,' said Howard. 'Mr

Bullerton, I mean. I've been trying to tell you, I…'

'My dear young fellow,' said **JB Undercracker**. 'I wasn't born yesterday you know. I can see you've been eating these lunches and I want to know why.'

'*Err*…' said Howard.

'Mmm?' said **JB Undercracker**.

'Well…' said Howard.

'Spit it out, mister,' said **JB Undercracker**.

'*You were inspecting them,*'
hissed Purvis, from the
lunchbox.

'What?' hissed Howard,
back.

'*INSPECTING THEM,*' hissed
Purvis.

'OF COURSE!'
shouted Howard. 'That's
it! I'm a Lunch Inspector and I
was inspecting them to ensure
they meet the appropriate…
um… whatsits…'

'Whatsits?' said JB
Undercracker.

'Thingamies,' said Howard.

'*Nutritional standards,*'
whispered Purvis.

'YES, THOSE!'
shouted Howard.
'The nutritional standard

thingamies.'

'AH!' said **JB Undercracker**. 'Now you're talking. This is a subject close to my heart.'

'Oh good,' said Howard.

'I owe you an apology, Mr Bullerton,' she said. 'I thought it was simply greed.'

'HA HA!' said Howard. 'Certainly not! Good heavens, no.'

'So, how did we do?' said **JB Undercracker**, winking. 'Did we make the grade?'

'And then some,' said
Howard, enthusiastically.
'The cold roast potatoes were
particularly fine.'

'Any left?' she said, and
Howard passed her one.

'Delightful,' said **JB
Undercracker**, swallowing
it whole. 'You see, food is
so important for the active

School child, Mr Bullerton, fuelling as it does both brain and body and ooh, that reminds me, it's nearly time for the

GRAND

SPORTS DAY

to begin. All the guests will be arriving soon.'

'AAGH!' *shrieked* Howard.

'Yes, it is exciting, isn't it?' said JB Undercracker. 'Now,

I need you to help me with one or two things, so put Lydia's lunchbox down and we'll get going.'

'I'd prefer to keep it with me, thank you,' said Howard, gripping the lunchbox **tightly**.

'Well you can't,' said **JB Undercracker**, wrestling it from him,

and flinging it into a nearby room.

'Come along, Mr Bullerton.'
She climbed onto the scooter and
shot off up the corridor, with
Howard trotting worriedly behind.
'**OUch**,' said the mice
and Russell, as the lunchbox
landed with a b u m p on the
floor of an empty classroom.
'**TOOT,**' went Ortrud,
running after them.

'What now, then?' asked
Mickey Thompson, rolling out
of the box. 'Shall we go and
have a look at the playground?'

'WE CAN'T!' **shouted**
Purvis, hurtling out. 'Didn't
you hear what she said? She said
the GRAND
SPORTS DAY's
starting soon and all the guests'll
be arriving and you know who
that means, don't you?'

'TOOT,'
went Ortrud.

'No,' said Russell.

'YES!' **shouted**
Mickey Thompson, leaping
up. 'IT MEANS MR
BULLERTON!'
'EXACTLY!'
shouted Purvis.
'MR BULLERTON!'
shouted Mickey
Thompson, bouncing around.
'MR BULLERTON! MR...'
'One moment,' said Russell,
holding up a finger. 'I thought
the roast potato man was Mr
Bullerton.'

129

'No,' said Purvis. 'He's Howard.'

'Howard Bullerton,' said Russell.

'Howard Armitage,' said Mickey Thompson.

'I'm confused,' said Russell. 'If Mr Roast Potato is really a Mr Armitage and not a Mr Bullerton, why was JB Undercracker calling him Mr Bullerton and not Mr Armitage?'

'Because she's confused

too,' said Purvis. 'You see Mr Bullerton's Mr Roast, I mean Howard's horrible boss and he sent us here to say he'll be the Guest of Honour, but **JB Undercracker**'s never met him and now she thinks he's Howard.' Purvis took a breath. 'Or Howard's him, and when he finds out about all the mess and the lunch inspecting and everything he'll be furious and shout at Howard even though it isn't Howard's fault, and

he'll be here soon so we need
to help but we haven't even
started making the appropriate
arrangements.' Purvis sat
down, **puffing**.

'What appropriate
arrangements?' said Russell.

'The usual things for a Guest
of Honour,' said Mickey
Thompson.

'Those being?' said Russell.

'Plinths, cordials, etc,'
chorused the mice.

'Oh,' said Russell. 'Those.'

'*Err*, Russell?' said Purvis.
'What exactly are plinths,
cordials, etc?'

'Nothing to panic about,' said
Russell, picking up a pen and
going over to a whiteboard.
'I'll take it point by point:'

*1. Mr Bullerton wants to stand
on a plinth, or platform of some
kind, so he's higher up and looks
important. We can build it using
bits and pieces from the shed
and the glue we've already got.*

'Any questions?'

Mickey Thompson waved his hand in the air.

'I thought the glue was for the vase,' he said.

'The vase has moved down the list of priorities,' said Russell. 'OK?'

Mickey Thompson nodded.

'OK,' said Russell. 'I'll continue:'

2. Mr Bullerton wants a jug of water and some bottles of something bright and sweet to put in it.

'Everyone happy?'

Everyone nodded.

'Good,' said Russell. 'And:'

3. Mr Bullerton wants a few

*extra bits and pieces along the
lines of the ones above.*

'Let's have some ideas,
please.'

'A great big cake,' suggested
Mickey Thompson.

'Some intro music,'
suggested Purvis. 'Or a flag. Or
a bunch of flowers.'

'TRUMPET,'

went Ortrud, joining in.

'Excellent suggestions,' said Russell.

'**TEN** great big cakes,' said Mickey Thompson. 'And a great big hat.'

'Right, I think that's enough, now,' said Russell. 'Time's moving on and we need to decide who's going to do what, including cleaning up the mess we've made – Mr Bullerton won't be pleased if he sees all that.'

Everyone agreed that Mr Bullerton wouldn't be pleased if he saw all that. They sat quietly for a moment or two trying to decide who was going to do what.

'Um,' said Purvis, after a while.

'Any volunteers?' said Russell.

'It's difficult,' said Purvis.

'Give it a go,' said Russell.

'Well, Ortrud's good at spraying water,' said Purvis, patting Ortrud's trunk, 'so she could clean up the paint we spilled in the Art Room, and all the footprints.'

'That sounds sensible,' said Russell. 'Will you volunteer for paint-cleaning duties, Ortrud?'

Ortrud **tooted**, and trotted off to find the Art Room.

'Not too much water,' called Russell, after her. 'What next?'

'I don't mind having a go at sorting out the cordials and flowers and stuff,' said Purvis. 'I like flowers.'

'And I'll make a start on the plinth,' said Russell. 'I enjoy building things.'

'What about me?' said Mickey Thompson. 'Shall I do some tidying up around the wall of lunch?'

'NO,' said Russell and

Purvis, quickly.

'Why not?' said Mickey Thompson, sounding a little put out.

'Because I might need you to help me with the plinth,' said Russell. 'It's a complicated job.'

'But,' began Mickey Thompson.

'*And*,' said Russell, 'I've still got to put the finishing touches to the egg machine, so you can help with that too; I can't manage it all on my own.'

'Oh,' said Mickey
Thompson. 'OK.'

'That's settled, then,' said
Purvis.

'As long as I can paint the
egg,' said Mickey Thompson.

'Hush,' whispered Purvis,
giving him a nudge. 'It isn't
your egg, it's Russell's. He
probably wants to paint it
himself.'

'You may paint the egg,
Mickey Thompson,' said
Russell.

'HURRAY!' said
Mickey Thompson, happily.
'But what are we going to
do about the wall of lunch?
There are noodles dangling
everywhere; someone might
notice.'

'He's right,' said Purvis.
'Someone might.'

'I know,' said Russell, 'but
without another pair of hands
I can't see how we're going to
manage to…'

'LOOK OUT!' **shouted**

Purvis, as there was a noise

from the corridor.

'SOMEBODY'S COMING!'

They all dived into the

lunchbox just in time as

the door creaked open and

someone came in. They all held

their breath as the lid of the

box flipped up and a furry nose

appeared.

'A dog,' said Russell.

'ALLEN!'

shouted the mice.

'There you are,' said Allen,
sounding relieved.

'He belongs to Mr Roast
Potato,' explained Mickey
Thompson, to Russell.

'Do I?' said Allen, sounding
surprised.

'So you're Allen Potato,
Allen,' said Mickey Thompson.

'Am I?' said Allen, sounding
even more surprised.

'Did you want us, Allen?'
asked Purvis.

'I was starting to feel a
little bit lonely outside,' said
Allen, 'so I thought I'd come

and find you.'

'Good timing,' said Purvis.
'The arrangements are taking
longer than we thought. Will
you be our other pair of hands,
I mean paws, I mean two pairs
of paws, and tidy the wall of
lunch?'

'Yes!' said Allen.

'Thanks!' said Purvis.

'*Err*,' said Allen.

'What?' said Purvis.

'It's just…' said Allen.

'Just what?' said Purvis.

'I don't know what it is,' said Allen. 'What is it?'

'A mess,' said Mickey Thompson.

'We'll show you,' said Purvis, hopping out of the box and leading the way, with Allen **trotting worriedly**, and Russell **trotting solemnly**, and Mickey Thompson trotting cheerfully behind.

'There,' said Purvis, pointing, as they arrived at the packed lunch storage area.

'Gosh,' said Allen.

'See what I mean?' said Mickey Thompson.

'**Oof,**' said Allen, as a dollop of something fell from the ceiling and *splatted* him in the eye.

'**Whoops,**' said Purvis.

'*Mmm!*' said Allen, licking.

'You'll be all right here then?' asked Purvis.

'Mmm,' said Allen, licking harder. 'Mmmmmm.'

So they left Allen doing a thorough job of the tidying up and set off to make the other arrangements: Purvis to find some flowers and cordials and things; Russell to build the plinth; and Mickey Thompson to paint the egg for Russell's egg machine.

'I've been saving that egg

for a long time,' Russell told
Mickey Thompson as he left
him with the tube of paint and
a brush. 'It has a particularly
pleasing shape. Make a good job
of it, won't you?'

'I'll do my best,' said Mickey
Thompson. 'Did you want it
to be red all over or can I do a
pattern?'

'It's up to you,' said Russell,
'but make it look distinctive.
Then all the people at the

GRAND SPORTS DAY

will notice it and be impressed.'

'Hmm,' said Mickey Thompson, once he was alone with the egg. 'Something distinctive.'

He studied it close up, and he viewed it from a distance, and he walked around and around examining it from every angle.

'Should it be spotty?'
he wondered.

'Or stripey?

Or checky?

Or with zig-zags?

Or flamingos? Or…'

'Ooooooh!' he said, 'I know.'

And, very carefully, Mickey Thompson started to paint.

GRAND SPORTS DAY

Part 2

It was nearly time for the

GRAND

SPORTS DAY

to begin and everyone was

feeling excited. The appropriate
arrangements were almost
ready, so Mickey Thompson
and Purvis went out to the
playing field to find Howard,
who was up a ladder hanging
bunting from a tree.

'Howard,' they said. 'Can
you help?'

'Mmm?' said Howard,
fiddling with a knot.

'It's the plinth,' said Purvis.

'I haven't been able to find
one, I'm afraid,' said Howard.

'Mr Bullerton will just have to manage without. He can stand on a chair or something.'

'He won't need to,' said Purvis. 'There's a plinth in the shed. Russell made it, but we need you to carry it out. It's too big for us.'

'Plinth? Shed?' said Howard. 'Russell?'

'That's right,' said Purvis.

'Who is this Russell?' said Howard.

'He's the stick insect that

lives in the School ,'
said Mickey Thompson, and
Howard tottered on his ladder.

'Careful,' said Purvis.

'The stick insect that lives
in the School has built a
plinth,' said Howard.

'Yes,' said the mice.

'You're having me on,' said
Howard.

'No,' said the mice. 'So will
you come and carry it, please.'

Howard sighed, and climbed
down the ladder.

'Lead on,' he said. 'I'm all agog.'

So they took Howard to the shed and showed him the plinth, which was made from pieces of wood and bits of box with a velvet cushion glued on top.

'Heavens,' said Howard.

'Isn't it lovely?' said Purvis.

'*Err*...' said Howard.

'Especially the cushion.'

'The cushion is a nice touch,' conceded Howard, 'but there

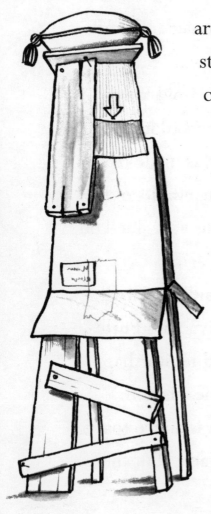

are issues of
stability to
consider.'
'How do
you mean?'
asked Purvis.
'It looks
as though
it could
collapse
at any
moment,'
said
Howard.

'I think it'll be safer to stick with the chair idea.'

'But Howard,' said Purvis. 'Russell's gone to a lot of trouble.'

'I can see that,' said Howard, 'but…'

'And Mr Bullerton specifically asked for a plinth,' said Purvis. 'Several, actually, so I don't think he'll be happy making-do with a chair.'

'Possibly not,' said Howard, 'but…'

'He'll blame you if he doesn't get one,' said Mickey Thompson.

'All right, all right,' said Howard, picking up the plinth and staggering back to the playing field.

'There,' he **puffed**, plonking it down. 'Now I must get on with this bunting. Everyone will be here soon.'

'Howard,' said Purvis.

'Mmm?' said Howard, fiddling with a string.

'Can you fetch the bucket of water?'

'What bucket of water?' asked Howard. 'Which bucket of water?'

'The one for Mr Bullerton to drink,' explained Purvis.

'I thought he ordered cordials,' said Howard.

'He did,' said Purvis, 'and I've got them – look.' He showed Howard a jam jar with something bright blue in it, a plastic cup with something

bright green in it, and a saucer
with something silver and
sparkly in it.

'Well, then,' said Howard.
'We're covered on the
cordials front.'

'But Russell said there should
be a jug of water to go with
them,' said Purvis.

'Did he, now?' said Howard.
'Full of bright ideas, your
Russell, isn't he?'

'Yes,' agreed Purvis, 'and
I couldn't find a jug, so a

bucket seemed the next best thing.'

'*Yuck,*' said Howard, sniffing the saucer. 'What exactly are these things?'

'Oh,' said Purvis, 'just… cordials.'

'And where did you find them?' asked Howard.

'Oh,' said Purvis, 'just…
around and about. QUICK,
let's get the bucket.' He
sprinted off and Mickey
Thompson sprinted after him,
so Howard followed, collected
the bucket of water, and
sploshed back to the
playing field.

'There,' he **puffed**, plonking it down next to the plinth. 'Now I must get on with this bunting.'

He climbed the ladder and began fiddling about again, while the mice hovered underneath.

'You're hovering,' said Howard.

'We need some more help,' said Purvis.

Howard *sighed* and climbed
down.

'Well?' he said.

'There are a few other bits
and pieces that need bringing
out,' said Purvis.

'Such as?' said Howard.

'Some broccoli, a book on
baking, a miniature violin and
an egg machine,' said Mickey
Thompson.

'I'm reluctant to ask,' said
Howard, 'but I think I'm going
to have to.'

'Well, said Purvis, 'the
broccoli's instead of a bunch of
flowers because I couldn't find
any, and the book on baking's
instead of a great **big** cake
because I couldn't find one of

those either, and…'

'It's got some very nice pictures in it, that book,' said Mickey Thompson.

'I'm so pleased,' said Howard.

'Especially the one on page 14,' said Mickey Thompson.

'And the miniature violin's for you to play as intro *music*,' continued Purvis, 'and…'

'Stop,' said Howard. 'What?'

'Page 14,' said Mickey Thompson. 'It had really **thick**

icing. *Really* **thick**.'

'Not that,' said
Howard. 'What was
it you said about intro
music?'

'For Mr Bullerton,'
said Purvis.
'Played by you.'

'I can't play
the violin,' said
Howard.

'It's only a
small one,' said
Purvis. 'There's

a sticker on it saying "*Designed for the Young Beginner, three years and up.*".'

'That won't necessarily help,' said Howard.

'No?' said Purvis.

'No,' said Howard, **firmly**.

'Well how about a triangle, then?' suggested Purvis. 'I found one of those too, and they're easy.'

'Triangle it is,' said Howard, checking his watch. 'And what was the other thing?'

'Russell's egg machine,' said Purvis. 'He's entering it in the egg race.'

'I painted the egg,' said Mickey Thompson. 'It's distinctive.'

'Yes,' *muttered* Purvis. 'It is.'

'Come on, then,' said Howard. 'You'd better show me where it all is.'

So the mice took Howard into the **School** and they all splashed along the corridor towards Russell's room.

'Everything seems rather wet,' commented Howard.

'Hmm,' said Purvis, worriedly, as they rounded the corner and arrived at the wall of lunch where, surrounded by empty boxes, Allen was curled up asleep on one shelf, covered in crumbs, and Ortrud was curled up asleep on another shelf, covered in paint, both snoring **heavily.**

'Oh dear,' said Purvis.

'Oh lawks,' said Howard.

'Bother,' said Mickey Thompson. 'There's nothing left.'

'QUICK!' said Howard, bouncing. 'We need to wake them up and get them out of here. I don't want to get caught by…'

'MR BULLERTON!' came a voice from up the corridor.

'JB Undercracker,' groaned Howard. He quickly positioned himself in front of Allen and Ortrud and stuffed the mice in his pocket as she whizzed towards them, with Mr Bullerton stomping furiously behind.

'WHEE!' shouted JB 'Undercracker, skidding to a

halt,
spraying
paint and
water
everywhere.

'Everything seems rather wet, Mr Bullerton,' she said.

'Yes,' said Howard and Mr Bullerton, together. Mr Bullerton glared at Howard.

'Now then, Mr Bullerton,' said **JB Undercracker**, to Howard.

'Me?' said Howard.

'You,' said **JB Undercracker**.

'*Ha ha,*' said Howard, nervously. *'Mmm?'* Mr Bullerton made a *growling* noise in his throat.

'It's the strangest thing,' said **JB Undercracker**, flicking her thumb towards Mr Bullerton, 'but this gentleman here claims to be a Mr Bullerton too!'

'Extraordinary!' said Howard.

'Isn't it?' said **JB Undercracker**, giggling.

'Not *claim*,' said Mr Bullerton. '*Am*. And not *a*,' said Mr Bullerton. '*The*.'

'Come again?' said **JB Undercracker**.

'I'm telling you I am Mr Bullerton, *ME*, and this man,' he pointed at Howard, '*HE* is an IMPOSTER.'

'No, no,' said **JB Undercracker**. 'He's an inspector.'

'*OOH!*' said Howard. 'Just look at the time. Don't you think we ought to be getting along to the Sports Day?'

'INSPECTOR?' **shouted** Mr Bullerton. 'WHAT KIND OF INSPECTOR?'

'A lunch one, checking up on the thingamies,' said **JB Undercracker**, 'and… err… oh dear,' she said, noticing the empty boxes for the first time. 'Mr Bullerton? What's happened to all the lunches?'

'What lunches?' said Howard, gazing around.

'The ones that used to be in these empty boxes,' said **JB Undercracker**.

'Oh, those lunches.' said Howard. 'Yes, I've been

meaning to speak to you about that.'

JB Undercracker and Mr Bullerton waited for Howard to speak.

'Now would seem to be a good time,' said **JB Undercracker**, after a while.

'*Err*...' said Howard.

'Mmm?' said **JB Undercracker**.

'Well...' said Howard.

'*You were inspecting them again*,' hissed Purvis, from the pocket.

'*What?*' hissed Howard, back.

'*INSPECTING THEM AGAIN,*' hissed Purvis. '*IT WAS A RE-INSPECTION.*'

'*Can't you think of anything better to say than that?*' hissed Howard, into the pocket.

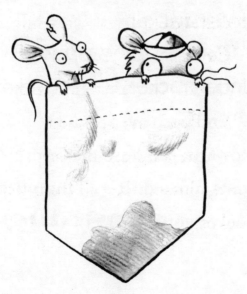

'*No,*' hissed Purvis, back.

'Right,' sighed Howard. 'Unfortunately, I had to conduct a re-inspection of the entire Packed Lunch Storage Area as a result of which all the lunches have now been confiscated.'

'Confiscated?' *gasped* JB **Undercracker**.

'And destroyed,' said Howard, 'because they were contaminated. It's all this water you've got **sloshing** around, you see. It makes things damp and unhygienic.'

'I suppose it does,' said **JB Undercracker**. 'You've been most helpful, Mr Bullerton.'

'It's all part of the service,' said Howard, and Mr Bullerton made another *growling* noise.

'I should get a plumber in if I were you,' advised Howard.

'And an ice-cream van,' said **JB Undercracker**, looking up the number on her phone.

'If you think it will help,' said
Howard.

'The poor dears have got
to eat something,' said **JB
Undercracker**, making the
call. 'They're going to be doing
a lot of running around this
afternoon.'

'They're not the only ones,'
said Mr Bullerton into Howard's
car, through *gritted* teeth.

'**EEK**,' said Howard,
ju^mpiⁿg.

'See you soon, Kev, I mean

Luigi,' said **JB Undercracker**, finishing her call. 'Now, we'd better decide which of you Mr Bullertons is going to be the Guest of Honour.'

'I am,' said Mr Bullerton, quickly.

'He is,' said Howard, equally quickly. 'The Guest of Honour is definitely him.'

'And Mr so-called Lunch Inspector here has kindly volunteered to take part in all the races,' said Mr Bullerton, with a **syrupy** smile.

'Eh?' said Howard.

'All?' said **JB Undercracker**.
'People normally choose just
one or two.'

'All,' said Mr Bullerton.

'That's the spirit,' said
JB Undercracker, slapping
Howard on the back. 'You'd
better go and get changed.'

'What?' said Howard.

'You'll find some little shorts
in the changing room down
there,' said JB Undercracker,

pointing. 'Get a move on, laddie. It's nearly time for the

GRAND
SPORTS DAY

to begin.'

She climbed onto the scooter and shot off up the corridor, with Mr Bullerton st**o**mping *smirkingly* behind.

'What am I going to do now?' groaned Howard.

'Put on the little shorts?' suggested Purvis.

'I don't want to,' said Howard. 'And I don't want to be in the races.'

'It'll be fun,' said Mickey Thompson, *brightly*. 'We'll cheer you on from the sidelines.'

'That makes me feel so much better,' said Howard.

'It might be best to go

along with it, Howard,' said
Purvis. 'Mr Bullerton's going
to be cross enough as it is
after all the business about the
Mr Bullertons and the lunch
inspecting.'

'Hmm,' said Howard.

'And anyway, it's just racing
a few children,' said Purvis,
trying to sound encouraging.
'You never know – you might
even win a prize. That would
impress him.'

'You're right,' said Howard.

'I'm bigger and faster than they
are: how bad can it be?'

He ran to the changing room
and put on some shorts, then
ran to the wall of lunch and
collected Allen and Ortrud,
then ran to Russell's room and
collected Russell, the broccoli,

the book on baking, the triangle, the mice and the egg machine.

'**Yikes,**' said Howard, staring at the egg.

'Do you think it's distinctive?' asked Mickey Thompson.

'**Yikes,**' said Howard, still staring at it.

'*Err*... QUICK!' **shouted** Purvis. 'I can hear a whistle. They must be starting the races!'

'**Yikes,**' said Howard, still staring at the egg.

'COME ON, HOWARD!'

shouted Purvis, into Howard's ear. 'If you're late you'll be in even more trouble.'

"Yikes!" yelled

Howard. 'You're right. LET'S GO!'

So they all **sploshed** quickly down the corridor and out onto the playing field, which was now full of ice-creams

198

and children and
bunting and guests,
and hoops and
scooters and
space-hoppers
and eggs and
all sorts of
other racing
equipment,
and over
seeing it
all sat Mr
Bullerton,
on his plinth.

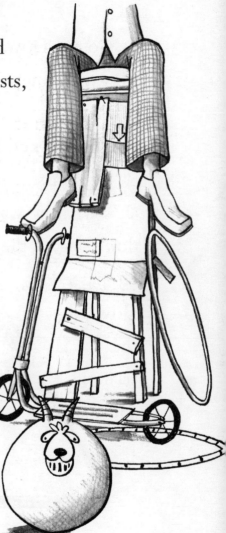

'Go on, Howard,' said
Mickey Thompson. 'Give him
his stuff.'

'Must I?' said Howard.

'Of course,' said Purvis.
'It's what he wanted. Oh, and
don't forget the intro music.'
He passed
Howard
the
triangle,
and

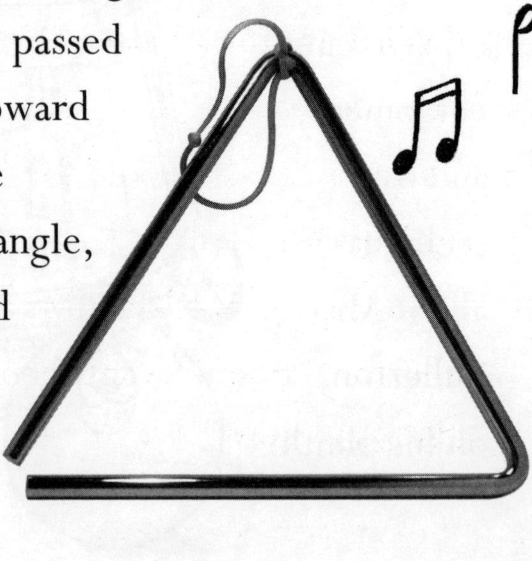

Howard went over to the plinth and gazed upwards.

'Well?' said Mr Bullerton, gazing downwards.

'Here,' said Howard, handing up the broccoli and the book on baking.

'What are these?' said Mr Bullerton.

'The things you asked for,' said Howard.

'No they're not,' said Mr Bullerton. 'I don't want them. Take them away.'

'*Intro music*,' hissed Purvis.

'Apparently page 14's well worth a look,' said Howard, tinging the triangle.

'Stop that *tinging*,' barked Mr Bullerton. 'Have you taken leave of your senses?'

'No,' said Howard. 'I don't know; probably; I just…'

'AND WHAT'S THAT THING DOING HERE?'

shouted Mr Bullerton, suddenly noticing Allen.

'*Ah-ha!*' said **JB Undercracker**, bustling up. 'There you are, Mr Bullerton. Ready?'

'Well…' said Howard.

'Feeling energetic?' said **JB Undercracker**.

'Um ...' said Howard.

'Wonderful,' said **JB Undercracker**, manhandling him away and over to the starting line, where a large group of children was waiting for the racing to begin.

'There he is!' said Mickey Thompson, excitedly, as he and the others watched from their spot on the sidelines.

'GOOD LUCK, HOWARD!'

shouted Purvis.

'He's looking a little bit worried,' said Allen.

'And he's still got the

broccoli,' said Purvis, peering.
'Maybe I should go and…'

'Too late,' said
Mickey Thompson, as **JB
Undercracker** gave a loud
blast on her whistle.

'RUNNERS
AT THE
READY,' she
shouted. 'GO!'

'Oof,' said Howard, as he was trampled underfoot by stampeding children.

'Whoops,' said Purvis.

'Ouch,' said Mickey Thompson. 'That looked painful.'

'Never mind, Mr Bullerton!' called JB Undercracker,

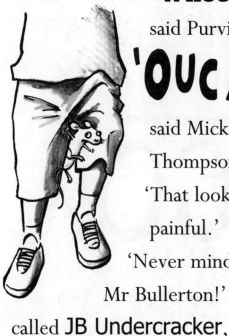

as Howard staggered to his feet and limped along. 'Better luck next time. Aaaaand SPACE-HOPPERS AT THE READY,' she shouted.

'GO!'

'Oof,' said Howard, as he was trampled underfoot by bouncing children.

'Deary-me,' said Russell.

'I can't bear to watch,' said Allen.

'You're doing marvellously, Mr Bullerton!' called **JB Undercracker**, as Howard curled up into a little ball.

'**A a a a a n d**

SACK-RACERS AT THE READY...'

'WAIT!' *squawked*
Howard.
'GO!' **shouted**
JB Undercracker.'

'WHUMPH,' said Howard,
as he was trampled
underfoot by jumping children.

'HAHAHA
HAHAHA!'
laughed Mr Bullerton, atop
his plinth. 'YOU'RE
USELESS, HOWARD
ARMITAGE. U. S. E.

L. E. S. S. USELESS.'

'Help,' gulped Howard.

'GO!' shouted

JB Undercracker, setting off

another one.

'TOOT,'

went Ortrud,

loudly.

'**Ooh-err,**' said Allen,
worriedly.

'*Squashed,*' said Mickey
Thompson, sadly.

'We must help him,' said
Purvis. 'Russell! What
shall we do?'

'I've got an idea,' said Russell. 'Tell him to ask for the egg machine race. It's slower; he'll be able to rest.'

So Purvis scurried over to where Howard was lying on the ground and whispered into his ear.

'Ugh?' groaned Howard.

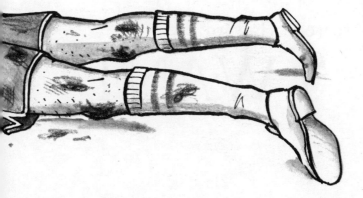

'*The egg race!*' whispered
Purvis. '*Ask for it now!*'
"Ugh-gug,' groaned
Howard.

'**Louder,**' whispered
Purvis, '*and with enthusiasm.*
Then you'll be able to rest.'

'EGG RACE,'

roared   Howard.

'I WANT

THAT EGG RACE NOW.' 'YES!' *shrieked* JB Undercracker, clapping her hands. 'That's my favourite. EGG RACE, EVERYBODY! START THE EGG RACE NOW!'

So everybody ran back
and forth finding their eggs
and their egg machines and
lining them up on the starting
line. Looking **hot** and
dishevelled, Howard
carefully positioned Russell's
complicated contraption next
to all the other complicated
contraptions and balanced
the painted egg on top.
Mr Bullerton peered down
from his plinth and eyed it,
suspiciously.

'*Distinctive*, isn't it?'

said Mickey Thompson.

'Extremely,' said Russell.

'We may have a problem,'

puffed Howard, arriving beside them as Mr Bullerton eyed the egg harder.

'Ah,' said Purvis.

'**A a a a a a n d ...**' said **JB Undercracker**.

'STOP!'

ordered Mr Bullerton.

Everyone **froze** as he clambered down from the plinth. Everyone gulped as he approached the painted egg. Everyone held their breath as he bent to examine it.

Mickey Thompson was right: it was distinctive, with two eyes and a mouth and a tongue sticking out and, underneath, the word 'BULLERTON,' carefully written in large and very red letters.

Mr Bullerton began to shake his fist.

'Howard!' *gasped* the Clumsies.

'GO!' *yelled* JB Undercracker.

'NOOO!' *shrieked* Mr Bullerton, as he was toppled by clattering egg machines and *splattered* with breaking eggs.

'**Aaaaaaaand...**' said
JB Undercracker.

'Howard?' said the Clumsies.

'Let's go!' said Howard. And
they did.

Coming Soon...

Make a Mess of the Airport